Ghosts of Darke County

A collection of ghosts' stories.

Rita Arnold

White Dog Books

Cover Design by Ron D'Allessandris

Library of Congress Catalogue

Card Number TXu 1-075-708

ISBN # 0-9788463-4-6

This book is dedicated to my husband Mike and to my very close friend Susie Weisenbarger. Because of their wonderful encouragement and support, this book was written.

Acknowledgments

I want to thank the Greenville Advocate for publishing some of the old legends just as they were handed down from generation to generation.

Also, a thank you to the Greenville Library for caring for the books and old newspapers from long ago and making them available to the public.

And thank you to my many friends who shared their stories with me.

Introduction

A lifetime fascination with ghost stories, the unknown, the unexplained movement of objects, the sounds that occur when you know that you are alone, these are just some of the reasons for my writing this book. Another very important reason is my love for Darke County and my family history and involvement in this county since the very early 1800s.

I am pleased to share with the reader my collection of stories and hope that they are enjoyable and entertaining. These tales are written only for fun, not to be taken as historical fact. I did change the names and some of the locations to protect the privacy of the current residents.

You will find that most of these ghost stories do not involve violence or harm to any person. Just some fun entertaining local tales involving the past and the present, great for retelling on a dark and stormy night.

Table of Contents

The Development of Darke County   1

1.	The Log Cabin	5
2.	The Headless Man	11
3.	Crybaby Bridge	15
4.	Friendly Ghost	19
5.	Werewolf	25
6.	The Stagecoach Station	29
7.	The Upstairs	33
8.	The Bookstore	37
9.	A Haunted House	41
10.	The Hallway	45
11.	The Family	49
12.	The Store	55
13.	The Pennies	59
14.	Have You Heard?	63

References   67

The Development of Darke County

Various tribes of Indians resided in the area of western Ohio before the formation of Darke County in 1809. The Indians traveled the land in search of food and shelter for their families. Many of the tribes existed peacefully, while others fought fierce battles over territory.

In the late 1700s the white man can to the western Ohio area in the expansion of America, looking for a place to settle and raise their families. The late 1700s found the leader General Anthony Wayne in the area and Fort Green Ville was built for defense. After hard fought battles and difficult times for the army and civilians, the treaty of Green Ville was signed with the Indians on August 3, 1795. Years later, around 1800, Darke County was surveyed.

When the new settlers arrived in the area they found large forested areas, vast swampland, and many Indians living on the land. Carving out a homestead meant not only taming the land but also existing with the Indians, protecting your family from the wildlife and the weather elements, and fighting disease with little or no medical knowledge.

A stockade was built in 1812 at what is now Greenville during the second war with England. The War of 1812 was followed by the defeat of Tecumseh and his brother the Prophet in 1813. A second treaty was then signed with the Indians on August 20, 1814.

For the next several decades, settlers' continued to come into the area, creating the need for townships and hamlets. Land was cleared and settlements were established. By the late 1800's most of the townships and hamlets were platted.

With the fighting that occurred in Darke County, man against man, and man against the land, the weather, the diseases, and the fact that it takes hard work creating a home in a developing territory, could some of the pioneers still be with us? Did they fight so long and so hard for the land that they did not wish to leave?

I am not saying that I believe in ghosts but some times an event will occur that is difficult to explain.

As a child I was scared of the dark and now I welcome the nighttime. I have spoken with many people about their unique and sometimes fun ghostly experiences. These are people from all walks of life, professionals, laborers, young, and old. These are people whom I have not paid to tell me a story. They voluntarily offered to tell me about an unusual experience. In fact, they seemed happy to find someone who did not think that they were crazy or strange. I have changed their names and the location of the buildings to protect their privacy.

Did you ever sit in your house or a building at night and think that you are alone – but you are not? Did you think you saw someone in the hallway? Were the lights suddenly turned on in another room and no one was there?

Did you feel the wind on your back? Did you feel a chill? Then these stories of Darke County are for you.

Join me as you meet some of the people of Darke County, the lady in the log cabin, the church clock that refuses to work, the church pew where two people became suddenly ill – 60 years apart to the day, the rural farm house where you can see a camp fire in the back yard, the house where you hear footsteps, and visit cry baby-bridge. These stories do not end with a "got – cha."

Should you believe these stories? I do not know. That is for you to decide.

God created the Heavens and Earth and when He was finished He looked around and smiled, and felt satisfied. He saw an area of land with tall trees protecting the fertile soil and giving a home to the wildlife, a land laced with creeks and streams full of water life. He was satisfied and said, here the pioneers will create their homesteads, raise their families and I will help them. He created Darke County, God's country.

1. The Log Cabin

Twin Township is the second oldest township in the county. It was created in the early 1800s and encompassed most of southern Darke County until future divisions of the county lands occurred and formed more townships. The land was thickly covered with mature trees sheltering the soil and protecting the wildlife and the men who came to settle the area. The Indians had long lived and traveled upon this land before the arrival of the white man. For years the Indians lived in harmony with the land, taking only what they needed and giving back what they could.

As in other parts of our country, this is fought-for land, man against man and man battling nature. The pioneers cleared the land to establish their homesteads after enduring many hardships. The settlers lived difficult lives, working hard to support their families.

In the early 1800's, a pioneer family named Rush came to the area to homestead in what is now known as Twin Township. They cleared the land of tall trees, using the timber to build a one room log cabin and the necessary outbuildings. After removing the rocks from the fields and plowing the soil, they planted their crops and a huge vegetable garden. Soon children were born to the Rush's, and the family continued to grow and prosper. Mr. Rush had become a very successful farmer and business man when it came time to sell his crops and the occasional livestock.

As the family continued to grow he decided to build a larger cabin; therefore, a two-story cabin was built which was most unusual for the times. This log cabin had one room downstairs with front and back doors, a narrow stairway leading to the one room upstairs. A sure sign of wealth for this area.

Mrs. Rush was known as an excellent housekeeper. She was constantly cleaning and caring for her house, taking pride in the fact that visitors could stop in to visit at anytime and find her house spotless. Her garden and her fine

chickens were always shown proudly to the visitors. Company was always welcomed at any time and often invited to spend the night, as travel was difficult and at times very dangerous. The
Rush family was well respected and reported to be as fine a family as there could be.

Around 1900, the Rush family heirs decided to sell the property and it soon began a journey though a series of landowners who were more interested in the farm land than in the cabin.

The cabin still stands to this day. For many years it was covered over with various types of siding, and soon people forgot that the small two-story house was originally a log cabin. Then for many years the house stood empty. One day the owner decided to tear down the house as it was in a state of near collapse. A contractor was soon hired to do a complete demolition job. Imagine the owner's surprise when it was discovered that the building was originally a log cabin! The owner then decided to restore the log cabin.

After much time and money, the owner finished restoring the cabin to its original design. On the first floor was a single room with a fireplace and narrow steep stairway going up to another single room. The cabin had a front door facing the road and also a back door leading to the garden and the outbuildings: a good homestead for the early 1800's.

Has Mrs. Rush really left or is she still there watching over her home? There are times when no one is in the building but the owner. He can be sitting in the first floor room reading when overhead he will hear footsteps walking back and forth across the upstairs floor.

On a warm, sunny day this author was sitting in the backyard on an old wood chair between the cabin and the garden. No one else was on the property at the time, so I enjoyed some time sitting in the sun listening to the birds and otherwise enjoying the quiet. Then I noticed walking out of the back door a petite lady dressed in a long dark brown skirt and a light brown blouse. Her hair was pulled back into a tight bun.

Ghosts of Darke County

She walked from the cabin's back door, heading towards the outbuildings carrying a basket on her arm, taking a few steps and then vanishing before my eyes. I quickly stood up and walked around the property but could not find anyone else on the grounds. What or who did I see? I was not asleep because I was holding a coffee cup in my hand at the time and I did not drop the cup.

A few months later I told the owner about my experience. When I finished my story, he just looked at me and smiled. He then stated that he had a picture which was given to him the day before. It was a picture of the original settlers, the Rush's. In the picture Mrs. Rush perfectly matched my description! Is Mrs. Rush still maintaining her home?

Rita Arnold

2. The Headless Man

In the mid 1800s, the Blizzard family settled in the northwest corner of Darke County, farming over 100 acres located west of what is now Hillgrove. They were farmers who cleared the land of rocks to plant crops, such as corn, wheat, oats, and tobacco. Also, they raised a variety of livestock. They attended the small local church in Hillgrove where they soon became active members.

Alfred Blizzard along with his wife and daughter farmed just north of Union City. They often traveled to Hillgrove to visit with family, friends, and to attend church functions. Alfred was known as a quiet man with a gentle disposition. His farm reflected his orderly and tidy nature. The buildings and the equipment were always clean and in excellent condition.

Rita Arnold

Beginning in around 1885 Alfred started spending more and more time in Greenville in the company of a Mrs. Rhodes, a prostitute in that area who was known to many people. On the evening of January 26, 1887, Alfred Blizzard, appearing to be intoxicated, was seen leaving Greenville in the company of Mrs. Rhodes. This was the last time that Mr. Blizzard was seen alive.

A few days later a young boy was walking along Mud Creek when he noticed a pair of boots in the water. The young lad thought nothing of this and went on his way. After all, people did occasionally discard unwanted items by throwing them into the creek. On the next day the boy was walking along the same area, and this time he saw a human hand sticking up from the water. The authorities were notified immediately. The body was then taken to the undertaker in Greenville. There the remains were noted to have a bullet hole in the left side of the head, as well as 18 hatchet wounds to the head were found, a finger was cut off, and an arm was broken. The body was positively identified as Alfred Blizzard, age 55.

Ghosts of Darke County

It was learned by the sheriff that on January 26, 1887, Mr. Blizzard sold his farm (unknown to his family) and had $1,500 cash on his person. Alfred then proceeded to Greenville where he became intoxicated and was seen leaving the town with Mrs. Rhodes. In February of 1887, the Darke County sheriff, Mr. Lecklider, arrested Mrs. Rhodes in West Virginia and returned her to Greenville for trial in the murder of Alfred Blizzard.

Since the late 1800s, there have been reports by people, who, when walking along the Mud Creek in this area, would see a strange sighting. The clouds would occasionally cover over the moon, but otherwise the moon would shine brightly making it easy for people to see a good distance. Off in the far distance a man would be seen walking alone, along the creek headed towards Union City.

What was unusual about this man was that people could see through him; and this man was headless. He was seen carrying his head in his arm.

Rita Arnold

Every sighting reported him headed towards northwest Darke County. He did not speak to anyone. He just looked past them and continued walking.

Is this Alfred Blizzard? Is he trying to go home?

3. Crybaby Bridge

Every county has a certain location, a mountain or woods, a creek, or a bridge that is connected to local folklore, folklore that is passed from generation to generation which sometimes changes or even improves with the telling. There are no books or songs about Darke County's special location, but every generation of Darke Countians is told the tale of Crybaby Bridge.

This story is about one of those old narrow bridges that a traveler finds on a little used country road. A road where you can only drive at a slow careful speed for safety reasons. A road that in years gone by was a dirt road used for wagon travel. Horses went at an easy pace because the road would rise and drop like old fashion ribbon candy.

And only one wagon could cross the bridge at a time. The bridge has been there for many years, first made out of wood cut from local trees. Then years later it was rebuilt with steel to carry the automobile traffic. The road was then paved with blacktop. The water under the bridge is only three to four feet deep, but the bridge does stand several feet above the water making for a long drop to the water.

One tale that is told is that many, many years ago, when Gypsies would travel through Darke County, this bridge was the scene of sacrifices. The old legend states that the Gypsies would throw unwanted babies off the bridge and into the cold water below.

The story that I was told when I was a child was about a mother and her young baby. As some good stories go, there had been a heavy rain during the day. That evening along with a fog that grew thicker and thicker, the rain continued as the mother drove home. She was probably nervous about driving the old car due to the weather and her concern about her young baby's safety. Only wanting to arrive home safe and sound, she gripped the steering wheel tighter and tighter and leaned closer to the windshield trying to watch the road.

Ghosts of Darke County

As the mother was slowly driving the car, she kept a good lookout for deer and other animals that might dart into the roadway. Soon the mother neared the bridge. She thought she saw something suddenly run across the road in front of the
car. She quickly slammed on the brakes, and swerved the car trying to miss the animal. The result was that she ran head-on into the bridge structure with such a strong impact that the mother was thrown out of the car and into the cold water below.

The local law enforcement and neighbors quickly arrived on the scene. They were trying to save the mother's life when they heard the faint cry of a baby from below the bridge but further down the creek. The rescue personnel walked down the embankment, looking long and hard for the baby but never finding a body. There was no baby to be found anywhere near the wreckage. Was the body carried down stream, or was it carried off by some animal?

Rita Arnold

There never was any evidence found of an animal or any other object being hit that night that could cause the car to wreck.

If you drive over that bridge at night, turn off the car radio, and roll down the windows, you just might hear the cry of a baby; a baby that no one can find. A cry of a baby wanting its mother. A cry that never stops. [1]

4. Friendly Ghost

During the 1960's and 1970's, Mary and her husband Bill lived in a two-story brick house built in the 1800's.

This house is like many of that era built in Darke County. It has a wood stairway going up to the bedrooms on the second floor, pocket doors leading into the dining room, wood floors throughout the house, high ceilings with dark wood moldings and wood trim around the doorways. There is a basement with walls made of stone. A kitchen was added onto the house in the 1900's, along with a detached two-car garage built behind the house.

A large woods and acres and acres of farmland surround the house, a house which is located next to the wooded area. Only the few residents living on the road and the occasional people out for a drive travel this road. People driving by see

19

a good solid house that was built to provide shelter for families for many generations. Bill stated that they lived with a friendly ghost who did not cause any harm to anyone, but did occasionally scare the family.

With Bill working the early day shift and his wife on the night shift, Mary would get everyone off to work and school and then sometimes she would lay down to rest. She enjoyed sleeping on the couch in the first floor living room. The couch was located so that the stairway was behind the person lying on it, who could still hear any noise coming from the area.

Mary was just falling asleep when she heard what sounded like a rolled up ball of notepaper rolling down the steps and stopping on the first floor. Just a gentle tap-tap-tap-tap and the noise stopped. Mary stated that she would lie down on the couch for a couple of minutes and then the noise would start again, tap-tap-tap-tap. After a few minutes Mary felt brave enough to open her eyes and sit up.

Ghosts of Darke County

Remembering that everyone but herself had left the house, Mary carefully looked around the stairway. No one else was in the house and no paper was found. She decided to stay awake the rest of the day.

Bill told of the time when he was alone in the house during the evening hours. Sitting on the couch in the living room, he was enjoying reading without the radio or television being turned on.

Hearing footsteps coming down the stairs to the first floor he called out to see who was there, thinking someone had returned home without telling him. No one answered his call. Bill got up to investigate and found that he was still alone in the house.

The children believed that all of the events began after a tombstone was moved on their property. The family found an old tombstone just outside the kitchen door where they wanted to put in a walkway, and they decided to move the marker to the flowerbed for decoration. Did this upset the spirit?

For years the parents would tell the children to unplug all the electrical appliances that they were not using. This was done for safety reasons because some of the house wiring was very old. Occasionally a hair dryer was left plugged in; but there were never any fires or over heated wires.

Time went by and soon all the children were grown and on their own. The house was sold to new owners. Bill and Mary informed the new occupants that some of the wiring was old and to unplug appliances when not in use.

The new owners slept with an electric blanket, but were careful to unplug the blanket every morning. The couple had no children, just one friendly dog.

Only a few days after moving into the house, the lady received a call at work that her house was on fire. Upon putting out the fire and saving as much as possible, the fire inspector carefully looked over the remaining structure. The fire department determined that the fire started because the electric blanket was left turned on.   Strange, the previous owners had accidentally left various items turned on or plugged in and never had and fires in the house.

Was the spirit unhappy?

Rita Arnold

5. Werewolves

Do you ever drive through the countryside and notice the various wooded areas? Do you wonder what is in the woods? I do. The landscape is dotted with clumps of trees and woods containing anywhere from a few acres to hundreds of acres. I always look at them and wonder how long have the woods been there and is there a story connected with them.

If you place a dot on the towns of Ansonia, Versailles, and Greenville and then draw a line connecting each dot, you will from a triangle. In this triangle there is a road that as you drive along, you come to a large thick wooded area that surrounds the road. In the middle of the woods you drive over a bridge that crosses a small winding creek. This creek always has a few feet of water and flows at a good rate. These woods have been around for generation after generation. No one has cut any of the trees down nor does anyone want to.

The legend states that these woods are a home to werewolves.

This story dates back to before General Anthony Wayne came to this territory, a time when the Indians lived in this area. Before the Indians battled the white man, they had to deal with the land, the weather, and the wild animals.

The tale states that along the creek is a small piece of land that borders the woods where the Indians would camp. On a night when the moon was full and bright, the air very still, the werewolves would come into camp in the dead of night. They would steal the elderly, the babies, the animals, or the people who were too weak or unable to defend themselves. All that would be left was a bloody trail as the werewolves had dragged off their prey.

The Indians would not hear a thing except the howls of the joyful werewolves as they ate their nighttime snack.

Ghosts of Darke County

As time marched on, settlers moved into the area. People who tried to homestead near these woods would suddenly disappear and not be heard from again. Did they get lost in the woods or were they taken?

As the years passed, a covered bridge was built over the creek to make wagon travel not only a little more convenient between the towns, but also to protect the horses and people from the werewolves. A trip in this area was dangerous only on a full moon night.

Years ago the covered bridge was replaced with a steel structure. Then people could enjoy a beautiful drive down a curving road with a bridge over a small creek surrounded by trees and see a peaceful quiet spot. A person would feel that you have found a little touch of paradise.

But, if you dare to drive over this bridge when the moon is full and bright, you could become a part of the legend. If you slow down the car and turn off the radio you just may hear the howl of the werewolves. In the distance you may hear the breaking of tree branches and the screams of the dead. And if you dare get out of the car, you may become part of their midnight snack. 1

6. The Stagecoach Station

West of Arcanum, in the 1800's, was a very small settlement on the major road from southern Darke County to the town of Greenville. On one corner of the crossroads sat a large house that was a stagecoach stop (some documents state that it was also a store) and opposite sat an old brick church that presently is a private residence.

Surrounding this location are homesteads, many dating back to the 19th century. North of this location is a cemetery that served the small community for many years. This settlement was much like many others that dotted this county during its early years and as the years passed the names of the residents changed or were lost with time.

This tiny community developed because of a need for travelers to have a rest stop on one of the main highways of the day as they traveled from southern Darke County to

29

Greenville and back home. Travel in the 1800s was slow and difficult as people moved by horse and wagon. An average of
eight to ten miles a day was a good distance over dusty, bumpy roads.

By the time a stagecoach arrived at this location, the horses were tired and needed rest, food, and water. The passengers were in need of food and a rest as well. The stop also provided rooms for a night's rest before the travelers continued their journey the next day.

Local legend has it that in the 1800s civil war soldiers traveling this highway stopped here on a Saturday for a night's rest. The next day being a Sunday, they decided to attend the church services. As they were leaving the church the soldiers were all massacred. Their bodies were carried across the highway to the stagecoach stop. There the soldiers awaited their families to claim the bodies or were buried in the local cemetery. The legend does not tell why they were killed. This is one of those local legends that not much is written about but many people know the story as it is passed down from generation to generation.

Did one of the soldiers enjoy his short stay in the community? Since that event there have been some interesting happenings in the former stagecoach stop.

How do you explain the clothes dryer starting during the middle of the night? Or the fact that lights in a room will turn on when there is no one in that room. The ghost does seem to have a favorite room since that is where most of these happenings occur. This is where the light and the stereo will turn on, even with no one in the room.

Sometimes the owner will get up in the morning and find some of the decorative plates removed from the wall and sitting on the floor. Is this the ghost's way of playing a game or is he saying that he does not like the plates on the wall? [1]

Rita Arnold

7. The Upstairs

A lady (I'll call her Mabel) lived alone for many years in Greenville after her children had grown, moved away and her husband had passed on. Mabel never wanted to move out of her house that had been home for more than 35 years. It was a well built two-story frame house, with a front porch, one bedroom downstairs, a wood stairway leading upstairs to two bedrooms, a tidy small yard, and friendly neighbors.

The children worried about their mother living alone in that house and often asked her if she wanted to move. Mabel never complained and wanted to stay in the house with the memories. Whenever the children asked Mabel if she was alright alone in the house, Mabel would just smile as an answer.

Mabel slept in the first floor bedroom. Her children thought this arrangement was good because Mabel would not need to climb the stairs every day. For some reason the children felt that something was going on; but they had no idea what the problem could be.

After Mabel passed away, her daughter Ruby had to settle the estate. Ruby and her son decided to move into the house until after the estate was settled. This would make it easier to sort through things and to care for the house. Shortly after they moved in things started to happen.

When Ruby and her son were alone downstairs, they would hear footsteps upstairs walking across the old wood floors from one bedroom to the other bedroom. Then there would be pounding on the upstairs wall. Ruby's dog would start barking wildly, looking up the stairway but would not run upstairs. Ruby would go upstairs and look around but never found anyone there. All the windows were shut tight and locked.

Then one day Ruby noticed that her dog was not barking but sitting at the base of the stairs and just staring up at the second floor. This happened on more than one occasion. No one was ever found upstairs. Ruby and her son noticed the upstairs furniture was being moved around.

Shortly after this discovery, Ruby's son moved out and her nephew joined her; but he did not stay very long.

Were these noises the reason Mabel would not sleep upstairs? Did she never mention the noises for fear her children would think that she was crazy?

Rita Arnold

8. The Bookstore

Dave was a very likeable fellow. You might say he was made of good stuff. He was born and raised in Darke County, educated in the Greenville school system. As men from that era did, he served his time with the military. Afterwards, he returned to Darke County where he fell in love, married and began to raise a family. Dave was a professional person, with an excellent reputation.

Surely, throughout the years he heard the ghost stories about certain houses or locations in the county, but he never really experienced an event. In fact, he never gave much thought to the possibility of ghosts. He would just listen to the stories and then be on his way. Sometimes he would laugh at the stories or just shake his head at the tale.

Dave was always used to dealing with just facts and evidence.

One day while on a shopping trip to a mall in Dayton, Ohio, Dave decided to visit a bookstore. This was during the daytime and the mall was not busy. Noticing that no one was in the bookstore at this time, he decided to go in and look around. He was an avid reader and wanted to search for any new and interesting books. He checked his favorite section, the non-fiction, and then started to wander around the store. He came upon a section labeled 'Ohio and Local Interest.' These books were stored in the middle of the room on solid wood book cases.

While Dave was standing there reading the book titles and not touching anything, one of the books just out of Dave's reach suddenly fell of the shelf. Dave looked around and noticed that he was still the only person in the bookstore except for the clerk, who was at the register in the front of the store. Dave picked up the book and replaced it on the shelf. Dave walked around the book display thinking there might be someone else on the other side who bumped the display but found no one there.

Ghosts of Darke County

Dave returned to the Ohio section and began looking once more. Soon, again out of reach, another book fell to the floor. After looking quickly around and seeing no one else, Dave immediately left the store.

After Dave had left the store and resumed walking through the mall, he suddenly remembered the titles of the books which fell from the shelves. They were both books about Ohio ghosts!

Rita Arnold

9. A Haunted House?

Picture this, a haunted house right here in Darke County. Is this possible? Why not?

Located north of Greenville is a beautiful large two-story red brick Victorian farmhouse that sits back from the road at the end of a long winding dirt driveway. Drive in and you will see the wrap around front porch with white gingerbread needing a fresh coat of paint. The house sits high on a stone foundation telling you there is a basement.

Look around the property and you will see the house is surrounded by large maple and oak trees, which are probably older than the house. Behind the house are a couple of large worn barns with fenced in pastures. The barns and pasture fencing have peeling paint, boards have fallen from the fencing and the barns are starting to sag and lean to the east.

Rita Arnold

This house was built sometime in the 1880's and has had many families reside within its walls. Recently no one has owned the house for more then just a few years. Many of the residents reported the same events occurring during their stay.

Some people in the county know of the stories associated with the house, but they tell of many different reasons for the happenings. Is the story of the Indian woman killed on the property correct? Or is the story that the spirits of two spinster sisters who died on the property and do not want anyone living there correct? Could the story be true that a grandpa who lived there with his son's family is still protecting the children?

Different residents have reported a variety of sounds and unusual events happening in the house while they lived at that location. The ownership of the property would change but the strange goings-on would remain the same.

There were the times when the sound of a music box could be heard from the child's bedroom during naptime.

Ghosts of Darke County

The parent was sure that she had not started up the music box so she went upstairs to investigate.

As she entered the room, the music would stop. This happened several times until the child outgrew the need for afternoon naps. Many years later when the family would discuss living in this house, the daughter talked about remembering a man who would sit on the edge of her bed while she took an afternoon nap.

The families all agreed that at various times during the night, the lights would turn on with no one visible in the room. The faucets would turn on without any help from the residents. Then there were the times when the living room floors would shake when everyone was sitting in the chairs. As the vibrations would move through the room the objects in that room would slightly shake. This would continue as the vibrations made their way to the back door and on outside. It was as if someone very heavy was stomping through the room.

Rita Arnold

These families reported times at night when the beds would shake and the rocking chairs would rock back and forth with no one sitting in the chairs. Some of the owners reported the slamming of doors and the piano playing by its self (this was definitely not a player piano). 1

10. The Hallway

In the northwestern area of Greenville near the oldest part of the Greenville cemetery are many old two-story homes that have stood the test of time. Most of the homes were built during the first half of the 20th century.

These houses are the usual two story brick buildings with a basement. Most of the houses are surrounded by mature trees on a nice city lot. Some of these homes have had the same occupant for many, many years with very few changes to the structure. Other homes have had many owners throughout the years along with changes to the structures. A few of the older large homes have become rental properties and are divided into apartment units along with numerous changes to the buildings.

One particular large home was converted into three apartment units around the middle of the 20th century. There are two apartments downstairs and the top floor consists of the third apartment with its own outside entrance. Over the years many people have lived in the top unit. Usually it was a young person just out of school who was getting started on their own for the first time. Occasionally it was a single person living on their own a widower or divorcee.

As often happens with rental units, people come and go, never staying very long in one place. For some reason this apartment seemed to be the type of place were people did not stay very long. Usually six months to a year was the normal length of stay. Did the residents get tired of climbing the stairs or was there another reason for their leaving?

The current renter is a single lady in her mid thirties who has occupied this apartment for about four or five months. She loved the idea of living in an older house with the high ceilings, the pretty woodwork, and the large windows to let in lots of natural light. She decided the stairs would be good exercise along with her daily jogging.

Ghosts of Darke County

This lady is known as an honest person, not one for telling tales or making up stories. If she said something was so, people did not question her.

A month or so after she moved into the apartment, on a Thursday evening, she was walking down the carpeted hallway carrying an arm load of clean clothes to put away in the bedroom. As she neared the bedroom doorway she suddenly tripped. As a natural reaction she turned around and looked at the floor to see what caused her to trip. She could not find any tears or holes in the carpet. The carpet was tacked down very smoothly and had been installed shortly before she moved into the apartment. She thought no more about the trip and went on to put away the clothes.

A few weeks later on a Thursday evening she tripped again walking down the same hallway in exactly the same spot. Once more she checked the carpet. This time she got down on her hands and knees checking for holes or any rough areas. Finding nothing but smooth carpet she decided that she was just occasionally clumsy.

After tripping for a third time on another Thursday evening she told a close friend about what was going on in the hallway of her apartment. Carefully they checked the carpet and found nothing wrong.

Then they decided to speak with the elderly renter of one of the downstairs apartments. They carefully described what
happened in the hallway. The older lady who rented downstairs listened closely and started to turn pale.

All three people sat down on the porch. The older lady asked, "don't you know?" She then went on to say that a gentleman had rented the upstairs apartment for many years and just loved living there. He died very suddenly of a heart attack on a Thursday evening in the hallway. His body was found in the exact spot where the current renter kept tripping.

Now when the upstairs renter walks down her hallway on a Thursday evening she carefully steps over that spot. Sometimes she will say out loud "rest easy, I will take good care of the place."

11. The Family

Bill and Betty lived on the family farm all of their married life having inherited the land from Bill's family. In fact, Bill and his wife were the third generation of his family to live and work the farm. They had two teenage children along with a family dog and a cat.

The house had large thick woods to the east and crops were planted in the fields west of the house. Behind the home was a large very old wooden barn built about the same time as the house. Here the family kept a few cows, horses, and rabbits as 4-H projects for the children. The house itself looked like many other local farmhouses in the county being a two story brick building with a covered front porch and an enclosed back porch where most people entered the home.

Upstairs were three airy large bedrooms and downstairs were the front parlor and a larger eat-in country style kitchen. Under the house was a large basement with stonewalls and an uneven cement floor. Separate from the house was a small wood framed garage plus the usual assortment of out buildings that are found on a working farm.

The husband's company had transferred him to a better job that was located out of state. After much discussion by all of the family members they agreed this was an excellent opportunity for Bill and agreed to the moved. After the for sale sign was placed in the yard, strange events began to happen.

Early one morning the wife entered the kitchen to start preparing breakfast when she noticed a dirty coffee mug on the counter. Betty was always very careful about cleaning the dirty dishes every day and putting them away in the cupboards. She just never let dirty dishes set on the kitchen counter over night. The entire family always followed this household rule. When Betty spoke of this coffee mug to her family, they all denied using the cup. She guessed one of them was playing a joke on her so she put the incident out of her mind.

As time went on, the family would find other objects out of place in the mornings. This was obvious because the family was trying hard to keep the house tidy for when the realtor would show the house to prospective buyers.

It would always be small items like a rubber ball being left on the bottom step of the stairway, a foot stool by the rocking chair was moved over to the window which looked out over the backyard, a young girl's hair brush left in the rocking chair, or a child's book left by the fireplace. The book was always kept in a bookcase with glass doors. No one in the family had handled this book in months. All this time everyone in the family thought that one of them was playing a joke on the other family members.

One Friday evening the family went to visit their new town and to house hunt. When they returned home on

Sunday evening all sorts of objects had been moved but nothing was broken or damaged.

A coffee cup was on the kitchen counter, a book was on the small round top table with an antique oil lamp which had only been used for decoration by the family. On one of the upstairs beds, the covers were wrinkled as if someone had slept on the bed. There was even an indentation in the pillow where a person's head had laid. A rocking chair had been placed beside the window positioned as if some one had sat looking out over the pasture. The family had a neighbor who came to the farm daily to tend to the livestock but he did not have a key to the house.

When the family called the realtor to ask why the objects were moved, the realtor said that he did not show the house that weekend. Then the family called the neighbor to ask if he saw anyone in the house. The neighbor reported that he saw no lights on in the house. On Saturday afternoon he thought he saw the curtains move by the front window as if someone was trying to get a better view of the pasture.

Ghosts of Darke County

Now the family did become concerned. Every family member carefully helped to check all the rooms and nothing was missing or found broken. Who was rearranging their house? And why? Was a family ancestor visiting the house before new owners took over the property?

About a year after the family had moved, they came back to Darke County for a visit. One day they went out to the old homestead. The new owners were saying how much they were enjoying the old house.

After visiting for a while the family asked the new owners if they ever saw or heard anything unusual happening inside the house. The room became very quiet. Finally the owners told about the objects being moved about during the nighttime and the rocking chair that would be moved over by the window.

With a shy look on her face, the new owner's wife smiled and said, "one day when I was home alone I promised the ghost that if he would not move anything around I would leave the rocking chair by the window." Since that conversation nothing has been moved and the rocking chair has remained by the window. 1

12. The Store

Many of the buildings on Broadway in Greenville were built in the mid 1800s. There is a business on South Broadway that has been a drug store, a grocery store, a jewelry store, and currently is a fine quality craft store. This building is the usual long, narrow three story brick building, with lots of windows. The upstairs has seen various uses during the years as an apartment, for storage, and presently as part of the business.

Like other retail businesses this store has security monitors throughout both floors. Employees have noticed that occasionally a white misty shadow appears on the upstairs monitors. This is not the type of light that comes from a streetlight or the sunshine. One time the employees were watching the monitor when a male customer walked through the shadow. The customer the stopped and looked around as if looking for someone, then obviously shivered.

Other customers have reported seeing something out of the corner of their eye but never anything or anyone they could identify.

One night as the owner was getting ready to leave she carefully turned off all the upstairs lights. She walked across the street to get into her van to drive home, but for some reason felt the need to look at the upstairs windows. In one of the rooms the light was turned on. The owner had worked a long and hard day, she was tired and without much thought she said out loud "you turned on the lights now you turn off the lights." Promptly the lights went out!

One of the first encounters the owner had with the ghost was around holiday time. She was walking into the office after closing the store. From her office doorway she could see a decorated seven-foot Christmas tree. While she watched, the tree shook violently, as if a strong gust of wind just started.
All the windows were shut. The owner started toward the tree thinking that it might tip over. Suddenly the tree

stopped shaking and the owner stood still watching the ornaments sway back and forth.

There have been customers who stated that they felt someone was following them around upstairs but never saw anyone. One of the employees waited until after all the customers left, then went upstairs and told the shadow "you are scaring people and must stop it." The ghost has become less noticeable.

One day the store had received a huge shipment of new merchandise. The employees were busy the entire day pricing the items and putting them on display. The owner used a basket to carry the items up to the second floor. At the end of a tiring day she set her full basket on the floor upstairs with the idea of finishing the next day. She turned off the lights and left for home. The next day every item had been removed from the basket and was neatly stacked on the floor.

Rita Arnold

Someone once told the owner that a tire company used to be located in the building. She wonders if a former employee's spirit is still there. 1

13. The Pennies

When David and his family moved into their home, they had no idea what the future in that house would be like. The house was located in a nice older area of town. Like many homes built years ago, it was a two story well built frame home with mature trees around the yard.

David stated that the ghost leaves pennies all over the house, but the favorite locations are the front hallway and the upstairs hallway and bedrooms.

Soon after moving into the house, David started finding the pennies. He asked his son if he was leaving the money and why. The teenager denied any involvement. When the son was away serving in the Navy, the pennies continued to appear.

One night the children were at sleepovers. It was just David and his wife in the house. During the night they both woke up suddenly. After a few minutes they heard a penny drop to the floor, spin and roll.

Over a period of time the family collected enough pennies to finance a vacation!

Other events occurred in that house. When David's family moved into the house, the bathroom had a tub with the old style claw feet and old faucet handles. There were times when no one was in the bathroom but the water in the tub would start to run. After the family remodeled the bathroom, including new fixtures, the water was not mysteriously turned on.

When David talked to the previous owners of the house, they reported they experienced some of the same events. The former owner told about the attic door. On the second floor was a door that opened to a stairway going up to the attic that they would find open. This door had a deadbolt lock. Her children denied any involvement in opening the door. Finally she yelled at the ghost to leave the door shut. She never found the door standing open again! After David's family moved in, the door had been found open many times.

David stated that the events did not happen every night nor was there any set routine to the pennies. Also, his family had never had any bad incidents with the ghost. He did say that some of their friends are uneasy about spending time in the house. 1

Rita Arnold

14. Have You Heard?

In Greenville there have been reports of a young Indian girl walking around Water Street, seen only at night near a boulder that marks the spot where she was reported to be buried. The story is that soldiers from Fort Greenville assaulted the young girl who later committed suicide.

In Arcanum there was an antique store located in an old two story brick building. The business used both the first and second floors. Customers of the store reported going up the stairs to the second floor and finding a lady in a rocking chair by the window watching the street. She was dressed as one would in the late 1800's wearing a long skirt, long sleeve blouse, and her hair pulled back in a tight bun. Who was she? Why did she sit by the window?

In Twin Township there is a house about 15 years old that was built near a foundation of an old outbuilding or a small house. Why do the lights turn on when no one is in the room? Why do the owners occasionally see a dark shadow move down the hallway? And why is there a camp fire seen in the field behind their house?

Do you know there is a two story brick house in Arcanum where the upstairs closet door refuses to remain shut?

References: Chapter 3 Crybaby Bridge

1. "Believe in Ghosts and Haunted Houses? It's All in the Spirit of Things" *The Early Bird, (October 26, 1977)*

Chapter 4 Friendly Ghost
1. "A Full-Moon Night Brings Them Out" *The daily Advocate,* (October 27, 1994)

Chapter 6 The Stagecoach Station
1. "Believe in Ghost and Haunted Houses? It's All in the Spirit of Things" *The early Bird*, (October 26, 1977)

Chapter 9 A Haunted House
1. "Believe in Ghost and Haunted Houses? It's All in the Spirit of Things" *The Early Bird,* (October 26, 1977)

Chapter 11 The Family
1. "Darke County Has Friendly Ghost" *The Daily Advocate*, (October 29, 1994)

Chapter 12 The Store
1. "The Store They Call 'Enchanted'" *The Darke County Profile,* (October, 2001)

Chapter 13 The Pennies
1. "Spirit picks up tab for Shahan Family Vacation" *The Early Bird*, (October 9, 1994)

www.ingramcontent.com/pod-product-compliance
Lightning Source LLC
Chambersburg PA
CBHW020641130626
46552CB00003B/1344